NICKY THE GNOME
AND THE LOST SOCKS

MAGGIE PACZEK

Matador
9 Priory Business Park,
Wistow Road, Kibworth Beauchamp,
Leicestershire. LE8 0RX
Tel: 0116 279 2299
Email: books@troubador.co.uk
Web: www.troubador.co.uk/matador
Twitter: @matadorbooks

ISBN 978 1800461 659

British Library Cataloguing in Publication Data.
A catalogue record for this book is available from the British Library.

Typeset in 16pt Minion Pro by Troubador Publishing Ltd, Leicester, UK

Matador is an imprint of Troubador Publishing Ltd

To the wonderful children and dedicated staff of Walkergate Nursery School.

To my lovely grandchildren, Isobel, Alfie, Fergus and to Seve to who prompted Grandma to come up with Nicky the Gnome.

And thank you to amazingly talented Misia for her magical illustrations.

Nicky the Gnome lived with his family in a toadstool house in the woods.

Nicky's dad worked through the night lighting the woodland lanterns so that hedgehogs, rabbits and mice could find their way home. His mum bought fur from the rabbits and made warm clothes to sell to the gnomes in winter. Nicky's brothers and sisters collected berries and nuts. They were all busy gnomes, except for Nicky!

Nicky was lazy. He did nothing at all! He would not help his brothers and sisters in the woods, and he wouldn't even play games with the other gnomes. Lazy Nicky only liked to sleep! He crawled out the house, found himself a nice corner in the trees, curled up and had a snooze. This was easy in the summer when it was warm but when winter came and the frost sparkled and the cold wind blew, Nicky was not a happy gnome. He was a chilly gnome.

One winter's day, as Nicky scurried through the woods looking for a comfy spot to sleep, he noticed a little garden surrounding a house where some children lived. On the ground he spotted something red that had blown off the washing line. Nicky bent down and picked it up. It was a small sock and it felt very soft. Nicky tried it on, he wriggled his body down inside until his head stuck out of the top. It fitted perfectly and was just right for a sleeping bag! No one was around so Nicky tied the sock around his tummy under his gnome's jacket and he ran quickly out of the garden.

It was getting dark as Nicky set off for home. On the way, he had a sudden worrying thought. He couldn't take his sleepy sock into the house. His mum would see it and as gnomes don't wear socks, she'd know that he'd stolen it! He would have to hide it somewhere!

Nicky looked up into the forest and had an idea. He scrambled up the nearest tree, into the branches and tucked his sock away where no one else would see it. Feeling very pleased with himself, lazy Nicky ran all the way home.

The next day Nicky went out early to find his hidden sock. He had a quick nap to try it out and he woke with the idea that what he really needed were more socks to hide throughout the woods.

Nicky ran back to the little house to see if there were any more socks on the washing line. He was out of luck. No socks on the line, so Nicky decided to go inside the house on a sock hunt.

The front door was shut, so he breathed in and squeezed through the letter box. He tiptoed quietly through the empty house and he found his first sock behind the settee. This was a good game and Nicky was greedy. He collected even more socks. Some were under the bed; some were in the toy box. One was left in the washing machine and Nicky found three in the dog basket! Nicky gathered them up and hid them throughout the woods, so he always had somewhere warm to sleep.

Christmas time approached. The gnomes collected moonbeams for fairy lights and sprigs of holly to decorate their toadstool homes. Mum was working all night to make Christmas outfits for gnomes. Nicky did not help them; he was much too busy hatching up a clever plan. Nicky knew that children hung socks up for Santa to fill with presents. Now that he had a sock, he would go to the children's house and hang up one of his sleepy socks for Santa!

On Christmas Eve, Nicky went to bed early and pretended to snooze. He lay very still until the Gnome family was fast asleep. He sneaked out and ran to the little house. Again, Nicky squeezed through the letter box and plopped down onto the door mat inside. He crept into the living room and hung his sock next to the children's socks on the fireplace. Nicky hid behind the settee and waited for Santa. He was just dozing when he heard sleigh bells overhead. He peeped out and watched breathlessly as Santa came down the chimney with a loud thump! Santa took two brightly wrapped parcels from his sack and carefully put them into the children's socks. When he came to Nicky's sock, he stroked his beard and gave a big sigh. Santa reached in his sack, brought out a pen and paper and carefully wrote a note which he put it in Nicky's sock.

As soon as Santa had gone, Nicky rushed to the fireplace and grabbed his sock. He looked inside. No present, just a note. This is what it said.

Dear Nicky

I am so sorry that I cannot leave you a present. This is not your sock and I know that you stole it.

Santa

Tears trickled down Nicky's face as he read the note. He felt sad and ashamed. Nicky did some serious thinking, he needed to change his ways!

And from that moment, Nicky stopped being lazy. He made his bed and did all the washing up. He helped his brothers and sisters collect nuts and berries and as a treat on some nights his dad let him stay up late and help light the Fairy lanterns.

As for the stolen socks. Nicky thought of some good ways of using them. He gave some to the mice for blankets and he left some in the woods for children who got wet feet splashing in puddles.

Nicky is a happier Gnome now. He has lots of friends and might just get a present from Santa next Christmas.

Lightning Source UK Ltd.
Milton Keynes UK
UKHW050711251120
374042UK00002B/68